M and M

and the
HAUNTED HOUSE GAME

OTHER YEARLING BOOKS YOU WILL ENJOY:

M and M

and the
HAUNTED HOUSE GAME

by Pat Ross · pictures by Marylin Hafner

An *I Am Reading* Book

A Yearling Book

Published by
Dell Publishing Co., Inc.
1 Dag Hammarskjold Plaza
New York, New York 10017

Yearling ® TM 913705, Dell Publishing Co., Inc.

ISBN: 0-440-45544-8

Reprinted by arrangement with Pantheon Books, a division of
Random House, Inc.

Printed in the United States of America

January 1982

10 9 8 7 6 5 4

CW

For Erica
and for her friend Diana
P.R.

For Donna
M.H.

CHAPTER ONE

Mandy and Mimi,
the friends M and M,
were having a boring day.
The King Kong puzzle
with one hundred pieces
was much too easy.
"Boring," said Mandy.

The markers were old and dry.

"Yuck," said Mimi.

And the games

were the most boring of all.

They tried to think

of a really good game.

"Checkers!" cried Mandy.

"I always love checkers."

"But you always win," said Mimi.

"So that makes checkers boring
for one of us."

Suddenly, they thought of a game

that wasn't a board game,

or a card game,

or a puzzle game,

or a word game.

They had played this game before.

And they knew

it was never ever boring.

"The Haunted House Game!"

they shouted.

And shivers ran up and down

their spines.

First they made creepy spiders—
black widows,
deadly scorpions,
and hairy tarantulas.
"Make them awful!" said Mimi.
And they did.

When the spiders were ready,
Mandy and Mimi taped them
all over the wall.

"We need bat blood," said Mimi.
Mandy's red paint
was thick and lumpy.
"Perfect!" cried Mimi.
"Disgusting!" cried Mandy.

They made signs for the door.

One that said:

And one that said:

And one that said:

They made ghosts
with marshmallow heads.
Mimi's dog Maxi
always tried to eat them
so they hung the ghosts high.
The room was finally ready.

"I'm going to be the Bride of Dracula,"
said Mimi.
And she made scars on her face
with sticky, wet gum.

"Kiss me, Dog of Dracula!"
Mimi told Maxi.
But Maxi just walked away.

"I'm going to be the ghost
who haunts the house," said Mandy.
"I'll scare people
right down to their toes!"
So Mandy pulled the sheet
off her bed.
Then Mimi helped
wrap the sheet around her.
"How do I look?" asked Mandy.
"Spooky," said Mimi.
"Now let's find somebody to scare."

Sometimes they scared the twins
across the hall.
But the twins
were taking their afternoon nap.

The very best person to scare
was Fred the handyman.
Fred always rolled his eyes way back,
threw up his arms, and cried,
"Help! The place is haunted!"
But they hadn't seen Fred all day.

"There's nobody fun to scare," said Mandy.
"Let's practice anyway," said Mimi.
So they snorted and howled and coughed,
and even burped—if they could.

Suddenly, Maxi barked and growled
and wouldn't stop.

"Hey, we scared *somebody*!" said Mandy.

"Now for the next spooky part."

It had to be as dark as night.

That was the rule.

So they pulled down the shades.

And they turned out the light.

CHAPTER TWO

The room was very dark.
Maxi thought it was bedtime.
He went right to sleep.
Everything was very quiet,
except for Maxi snoring.

Then Mandy whispered,

"Time for the scary noises part."

Mandy had five hundred pennies

in a bag tied tight.

The bag went *plunk*

when she dropped it on the floor.

"That's not scary," said Mimi.

So Mandy opened the door
and slammed it so hard—

that the room shook.

But that was not scary either.

Then Mandy and Mimi made
shivery sounds and terrible faces
and dreadful noises.

But the house
did not seem haunted at all.

"We couldn't even scare a mouse,"
said Mimi.
Mandy and Mimi began to think
the Haunted House Game was boring, too.
Then all of a sudden,
they heard a noise.
It was a banging noise.

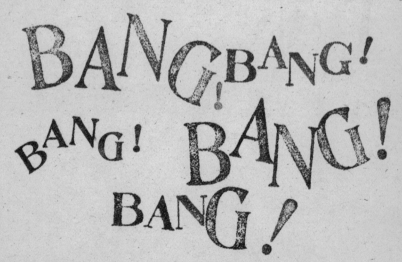

"What's that?" cried Mimi.
"It's not one of *our* noises," said Mandy.

Then the noise stopped.

"It was just getting good,"

said Mandy.

But then, the noise started again.

BANG!
BANG BANG!!

It got louder and louder.

And closer and closer.

Mandy and Mimi

looked around the room.

It seemed much darker than before.

The ghosts wiggled on their strings.

The spiders began to move.

And bat blood was everywhere.

"Who's there?" called Mandy.

"Who's there?" called Mimi.

WHO'S THERE?

CHAPTER THREE

The noise got louder and louder.

It came closer and closer.

Then, all of a sudden, it stopped.

"Look!" screamed Mandy.

A huge shadow—a monster shadow—
was right outside the window!

The monster shadow was very still—
too still.

The room was very quiet—
too quiet.

"What *is* it?" whispered Mimi.

"And what's it going to do?"

"Don't just stand there,"

said Mandy.

"Turn on the light."

"It's *your* room," said Mimi.

"So *you* turn on the light."

"We'll do it *together*,"

said Mimi.

So together

they crossed the dark room.

Together

they hunted for the light switch

in the dark.

Together

they felt along the wall

in the dark.

Suddenly,
something hairy and sticky
grabbed Mandy's arm.
Mandy screamed.

Just then, something soft and creepy
fell on Mimi's head.
Mimi screamed.

A paper spider
stuck to Mandy's arm.
A marshmallow ghost
sat on Mimi's head.
They looked at each other
and began to giggle.

Then the noise started up again
and they remembered
the *real* scary thing.
Quickly, they found the light.
Click!

The room was bright now.
They ran to the window
and grabbed the shade.

Up it flew
to the top of the window.
Zip!

Out came Maxi
from under the bed,
growling and barking
at the window.

And there stood the monster,
looking right into the room.
"Hey!" the monster shouted.
"What's going on in there?"

Then the monster smiled.

"Fred!" cried Mandy.

"Fred!" cried Mimi.

"Boo!" said Fred the handyman
who was fixing leaks in the old brick wall.
Bang, bang, bang went his hammer.

"I knew all along it was only him,"
said Mimi.

"Me, too," said Mandy.

"I knew it was Fred."

Then they waved to Fred.

They made scary faces at him, too.

Fred made faces right back

at the creepy Bride of Dracula and

the awful, spooky ghost.

Then Fred waved good bye.

And he moved down the wall

and out of sight.

But they could still hear him work.

BANG! BANG! BANG!

Now the game was over.

Mimi peeled the gum off her face.

Mandy put the sheet
back on her bed.

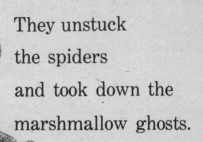

They unstuck
the spiders
and took down the
marshmallow ghosts.

They saved the signs
for next time.
And they threw away
the bat blood.

Finally, it was time to eat
the marshmallow ghosts.
Mandy and Mimi filled their cheeks
with ghost heads.
They gave the hard ones to Maxi.
"I wasn't scared," said Mandy.
"I wasn't either," said Mimi.

Then they hugged each other hard.

Because they both knew better.

And they also knew

that the Haunted House Game

was *still* the best game of all.

And NEVER EVER boring.

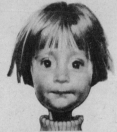